ADVENTURES OF A ZOMBIE

BOOKS KID

Bern, the zombie who wants to take over the world!

WITHDRAWN

Silver Dolphin Books
An imprint of Printers Row Publishing Group
A division of Readerlink Distribution Services, LLC
9717 Pacific Heights Blvd, San Diego, CA 92121
www.silverdolphinbooks.com

404 éditions
c/o Édi8
92 avenue de France
75013 Paris, France
https://www.lisez.com/404-editions/24

ISBN: 978-1-64517-683-1
Manufactured, printed and assembled in Guangzhou, China.
First printing January 2021 GD/01/21
25 24 23 22 21   1 2 3 4 5

ADVENTURES OF A ZOMBIE

BOOKS KID

Bern, the zombie who wants to take over the world!

Written by *Books Kid*
Introduction by *Aypierre*
Translated from the French by *Daria Chernysheva*
Illustrated by *Elliot Gaudard*

Silver Dolphin

INTRODUCTION BY AYPIERRE

Ah, the zombie . . . the most famous monster in movies and video games! These zombies can be the result of a forbidden experiment, an ancient curse, or a major epidemic. They always pose a deadly threat, even to trained survivors!

So it was to be expected that a game as successful as Minecraft would include its own version of the hungry, drooling undead—and that the poor, lonely player would have to fight these hostile zombies on top of everything else.

As for me, I openly confess that I dread these walking corpses. The problem with zombies is not only that they're disgusting: it's that they are also EXTREMELY persistent! Sure, they'll probably never win any points in the style or creativity departments. But we can acknowledge that zombies are *very, very* determined.

The zombie is certainly not the smartest of adversaries (which is funny, if you consider how a zombie's diet consists mostly of fresh brains!). But the zombie is definitely the most stubborn enemy you will ever come across.

In my many adventures, whether playing by myself or in your company, I have been able to observe Minecraft's zombies very closely, as well as experience their many determined attempts to devour me whole. With time, I learned to be so afraid of zombies that I would listen very carefully whenever I went out at night. I was terrified of hearing the zombies' distinctive growl. Before you call me a scaredy-cat, think about it: being blown to pieces by a creeper is not a great end, but that's nothing compared to being eaten alive by a mob of starving, brainless zombies! This isn't only painful-worse, it's embarrassing!

So it was with great curiosity that I devoured the misadventures of Bern the Destroyer (as he likes to be called). Bern's (sometimes) desperate attempts to organize and train his mob of fellow zombies are evidence of the legendary determination of zombies. I confess that I laughed far more than I screamed while reading this zany story. The more I read, the more I said to myself: it's a good thing zombies are stupid, otherwise they'd surely be able to take over the world!

I hope you enjoy this adventure as much as I did. In the meantime, keep an eye on your brain! **GRAAAAH!**

EDITOR'S NOTE

We don't know much about the Minecraftian Dark Ages, a time period that lasted about five hundred years. Few documents have survived from this time, and according to historians, this is due to a terrible zombie attack that had nearly wiped out Minecraftian civilization. Details about the Battle of Minecraftian Village Number 23 have been lost in the mists of time. All we truly know is that the village was destroyed.

Given the lack of evidence, there was great excitement when a document was discovered in the depths of the archives of the Central Library of Minecraftia when the old building was being torn down to make room for a new one. The text was very nearly thrown out with the trash, but it was saved by a young and quick-thinking librarian.

This diary is a rare find. It gives us a new look into the time period we call the Dark Ages.

DAY 1

Me? I'm (Bern) But people call me Bern the Destroyer. Or Bern the Mighty.

Or Mr. Bern, the Great Overlord. Or sometimes: "Aargh! Aargh! Get off me!" if they're being very rude. I don't get why people can't just hold still when I'm eating their brains.

I am the leader of the biggest zombie army that Minecraftia has ever seen. It took me many, many years to build my army and unite hundreds of the undead, who are all under my command today. You'd think it would be easy to gather zombies: we are social creatures, after all. When one zombie goes somewhere, the others follow. It's a natural instinct, hanging out with those who are the same as us. I like to think we zombies travel in groups just because we're very friendly, but, to be honest, it's also because we want to make sure we don't miss out on any juicy brains.

So it's not the most difficult thing in the world to get a bunch of zombies together. No, the greatest challenge is trying to transform an undead mob into a mighty war machine. You see, zombies aren't exactly geniuses. You tell them to go left, and maybe they'll put one hand out to the left, but the rest of the body goes right, or forward, or backward, or stays in the same spot and turns in a circle. . .Basically, zombies do everything except what you want them to do. They bump into each other, or else they fall over each other and don't bother to get back up again. They're happy to keep lying on the ground.

IT'S A MESS!

I would've pulled out all my hair, if my hair hadn't already fallen out long before, back when I first turned into a zombie. Mind you, I didn't have a lot of hair to begin with. Villagers aren't exactly famous for their amazing hairdos.

I don't remember much about being a villager. I think I may have been a librarian. That would explain why I enjoy keeping this diary. But I also could've been a weapon maker: I enjoy a good fight!

Either way, it doesn't matter what I used to be. Now I am a zombie, and I love it. All these delicious brains. . .

If only the other zombies weren't so dumb. It's a real challenge, creating an army to take over the world.

DAY 2

I HAVE TO FIND A WAY TO MAKE THE ZOMBIES WORK AS A TEAM.

Think of all the brains we could get our hands on, if we took the time to come up with an attack plan, instead of wandering all over Minecraftia and hoping to just stumble upon something to eat.

Today, I had the idea to disguise ourselves as villagers, so that we could take the Minecraftians by surprise. That way, I figured, the Minecraftians wouldn't realize we were zombies, at least not until it was too late. And by then we'd be munching on their juicy brains.

Have you ever tried putting makeup on a zombie?

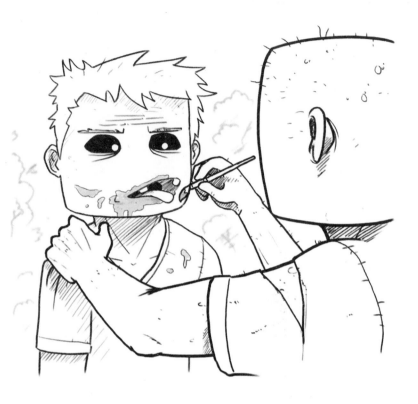

It's harder than you think! Zombies can't hold
still for too long. They can't keep themselves
from shifting and shuffling their feet. When I
tried to paint their faces a skin color, they
wouldn't stop moving, and the paint went
everywhere. Also, it's no use trying to paint
their mouths: they keep trying to eat the paint.

When I finally finished, the zombies looked even weirder than usual. Nobody would mistake them for villagers! But I had tried my best.

"VERY GOOD, MY FRIENDS! Off to the village. Don't forget: no moaning, no growling, and try to walk like humans. We have to surprise them if we want to eat brains for dinner."

As we were walking toward the village, I tried to encourage my zombies with a song that went like this:

"I don't know, but it's been said—"
"GRAAAAAAAH."
"Zombies all are really dead—"
"GRAAAAAAAH."
"I don't know but I've been told—"
"GRAAAAAAAH."
"Zombies like brains more than gold."

"Now be quiet," I said. "The village is right over there. We don't want them to hear us coming."

"GRAAAAAAAH."

I tried to make them quiet down, but it was hopeless: they continued to groan and make noise. So much for the element of surprise.

There wasn't a human in sight. Everyone was hiding in the safety of their houses. They must have heard us coming from a mile away.

"COME OUT!" I called. "We are Minecraftian travelers, and we are looking for someplace to spend the night."

I tried very hard to speak clearly, but it's difficult to do that when you're undead. I could be wrong, but I'm pretty sure I sounded more like a growling zombie than a talking human.

I went up to the closest door and knocked. I tried to look like a frightened Minecraftian seeking shelter, but no one answered the door. I thought I saw someone quickly look out the window. I flashed them my prettiest smile, but my teeth are rather pointy these days, so that could have been a mistake.

FINALLY, I DECIDED TO GIVE UP. MY
PLAN HAD BEEN A TOTAL FAILURE.

NO BRAINS TONIGHT.

DAY 3

Time to get serious. I have to find a way to train these zombies, to turn them into an elite combat corps.

I think I've been approaching everything all wrong so far. Take the great leaders from Minecraftian history: Alfred the Belligerent. Paul the Lionhearted. Benjamin the Conqueror. What did they all have in common?

They all knew how to motivate their troops. This is what I need to do. I must find a way to get the zombies to work together toward a common goal.

I had thought the idea of having as many brains to eat as you could want would be motivation enough. Clearly, I was wrong. But I've been wondering if there's another way to use a brain to get the zombies to work together.

And then, it hit me! What if we had an actual brain? I mean, a brain that was still inside a Minecraftian's head? A real, live brain?

The more I thought about it, the better I liked this idea. I'd have to be careful. Zombies want to eat any brain immediately, so I'd have to watch them closely until they finished their training. Once my soldiers were working well together, they'd be allowed to eat the brain. In fact, I'd join in! Even better, I'd personally lead my zombies to the table!

But until that happened, I'd have to protect that brain with my undead life.

The big question: How am I going to get my hands on this brain?

BEING A ZOMBIE LEADER IS SO DIFFICULT.

DAY 4

I have decided to enlist the help of one of my smartest zombies. Bruce.

He is one of the few soldiers I can count on to obey my orders. Well, perhaps he doesn't follow my instructions to the letter, but at least he knows the difference between left and right, and, compared to the rest of them, that's a lot.

"All right, Bruce," I said. "We're going to try and capture a brain."

"GAH?"

"No, we're not going to save it for dessert. We're not going to eat this one."

"GAH?"

"Don't be silly, Bruce. Of course I haven't become a vegetarian. We're going to use this brain to train my zombie army."

"GAH?"

"Well of course it's my army. I'm the leader, right?"

"GAH," agreed Bruce, nodding his head.

"Anyway, we're going to have to be very careful. I don't want to contaminate the brain. It will be of no use to us if it zombifies."

"GAH."

"I don't care if it smells really good. You will **NOT EAT THE BRAIN.** Got it?"

"GAH."

Now that Bruce and I were on the same page, the next step was to locate a brain we could capture. This was turning out to be harder than I thought.

It would be so much easier if we could go out in daylight. I tried, once. It's a good idea, but only if you like your zombies extra-crispy! I caught

fire and had to run to the nearest lake to put the flames out. Otherwise, I would be a pile of zombie ashes right about now.

Most Minecraftians know that these parts are swarming with zombies. So, at night, they lock themselves up in their shelters, which have very thick doors. Try as we might, hammering on these doors as hard as we can, we can never manage to break in. This is why I am building my zombie army. Once my troops have been trained, no door will be able to stop us. We'll eat all the brains we can find. Quite frankly, I'm starving. There just aren't enough brains to go around. Bruce has no idea how hard I'm going to struggle not to eat the brain we find. I will have to focus on the greater good: zombie victory!

Sometimes there are Minecraftians who venture into these parts, and I hope to come across one of them. We'll grab an adventurer and be on our way. That's all we have to do.

Bruce and I roamed all night, but we didn't find a single brain. Tomorrow, I'm going to send out the scouts. There must be some adventurers around.

DAY 5

I sent my best zombies to look for an adventurer, with Bruce leading the squad. I gave them strict instructions not to eat any brains they happened to find. Their objective was to find brains and report their locations back to me, so I could draw up a plan of attack.

My scouts were told not do anything to harm the brains. I would not be happy if they did, and all the zombies know what happens when I am not happy! You can still spot a few zombies walking around without arms from the last time I got mad. Their arms will grow back eventually. Still, it's a good reminder for my soldiers to do exactly what I tell them to do.

While my scouts were out searching for adventurers, I focused on training my troops.

"SOLDIERS! ASSEMBLE!"

Dragging their feet, the zombies arranged themselves into what they thought was a line. I looked at them and shook my head.

"How long have we been working on this?" I sighed.

I walked toward them and moved them into their correct positions. Now, at least, I had something resembling a line.

"All right, look to the zombie on your left."

Heads turned in every direction.

"YOUR LEFT, I SAID!"

I shook my head. "Fine. I'm going to make this easier."

I grabbed the remains of the paint that I'd used when I had tried to disguise my army. I went down the line, marking everyone's left hand with a large dab of color.

"Perfect," I said, once I was finished. "Now, every time you see paint, you'll know that it is your left hand."

"GAH?"

"Yes, your left."

"GAH?"

"No, for me it's my right."

"GAH?"

"That's right. Your left hand. The hand where the thumb points to the right. . ."

"GAH?"

I could feel myself getting angry. I grabbed the paint again and went down the line, this time turning each splotch of paint into a big letter L.

"L is for left. Now you don't have any excuses.

You all know which is your left hand! It is not the right one. It is the other one."

I sighed.
I was going to have
to give the order again.

"Now, I want you all to look to your left."

Heads turned in all directions, but this time, instead of continuing in confusion, the zombies examined their hands. Little by little, a rank formed before my eyes: zombies standing at attention and looking over their left shoulders.

"Good, good. Now, turn to the left. You're already looking in the correct direction. It shouldn't be too difficult."

At least, in theory. You'd be surprised how dumb zombies are, even with a big letter L drawn on their hands.

"Good, very good. I think that's enough for today. We will continue training tomorrow. Be careful not to wash off your L."

"GAH."

The zombies disbanded, dragging their feet, to go do whatever it is zombies do during their free time. Who knows.

Me, I don't have free time. I am too busy plotting to take over the world.

DAY 6

Bruce and his team still haven't returned as of this morning. I'm getting worried. Maybe they've been blown up by creepers, or eaten by wolves, or, even worse, transformed back into humans!

But a zombie leader cannot waste his energy worrying about his troops. If my scouts are gone, then so be it. I will have to come up with replacements.

I went to watch the zombies stumbling about our camp. **WHAT A MISERABLE BUNCH!** They lurched across the clearing, not caring if they ran into each other. I didn't feel that any of them stood out from the crowd.

Even so, I still needed to find my new second-in-command.

"YOU, YOU, AND YOU!"

The three zombies I called on stopped what they were doing and raised their heads in my direction.

"COME HERE."

They drifted over to me.

"Bruce is missing in action," I told them, "and I am going to need someone to replace him. One of you three will be the lucky zombie. I have a little test for you, and whoever does best will take Bruce's place."

"GAH!" said one zombie.

"Wait, I haven't even told you what the test is. But you get bonus points for your enthusiasm."

(I made a mental note not to choose that particular zombie.) "I need you to bring me some apples," I continued. "Whoever brings me the most apples will be my new lieutenant."

"GAH."

The three zombies slowly took off in search of apples. I didn't actually want any apples. Those things taste terrible. Nothing beats a nice brain. However, I wanted to see if these zombies could carry out my orders.

The overly enthusiastic zombie quickly lost all interest in the task. Just as I'd expected, he didn't have the makings of an officer. In fact, I wasn't sure I wanted him in my army at all! It's so difficult to find good zombie soldiers these days.

I observed the other two, who looked more promising. They had found an apple tree and wanted to begin gathering the fruit. But this, apparently, turned out to be far more complicated than I thought.

The zombies looked at the apples, but it seemed they couldn't stretch out their arms to pick them.

One of them hit the trunk of the tree, hoping to shake some apples loose. The other wandered about until he found a stick, which he used to try and make the apples fall.

The night was coming to an end. I could see the sun peeking over the horizon. All the zombies set off toward their shelters to spend the day. I had positioned myself safely in the shadows of my doorway, where I could keep watching the two zombies trying to pick apples.

When the first zombie heard everyone else going to hide for the day, he turned around and followed them.

The second zombie, however, remained at the base of the tree in an attempt to bring me as many apples as possible.

I watched him, still gathering apples, when a ray of sunlight struck him. What a shame he hadn't come back a few moments earlier!

SOMEONE SO DEDICATED TO HIS TASK WOULD HAVE BEEN A PERFECT MEMBER OF MY ARMY.

The other zombie came and put an apple in my hand.

"GAH?" he asked.

"Yes," I said. "You won. You will be my second-in-command, for the time being."

The zombie smiled, showing all his teeth. Then he went to his bed. I glanced at the spot where the other, dedicated zombie had stood. I shook my head. Oh well. This loss would serve as an example to other zombies. Let them try harder in the future.

DAY 7

My new lieutenant is called Bob.
I've decided I like him a lot.
He has a keen sense of humor
and tells me hilarious jokes.

"How many zombies do you need to change a light bulb? Zero. You don't need any, because zombies see in the dark!"

Okay, I admit it's probably not the best joke in the world.

But it came from a zombie.

SO WHAT DID YOU EXPECT?

DAY 8

With Bob at my side, it's easier to train the other zombies. He's surprisingly strict!

When I instructed the zombies to form ranks, Bob ran up and down, barking at them until they stood perfectly in line. I couldn't believe it. I'd never seen such a beautiful line.

IT HURTS ME TO SAY THIS, BUT I THINK BOB MIGHT BE A BETTER LIEUTENANT THAN BRUCE.

By this point, the paint on the zombies' left hands had washed away and I didn't have any more paint. I wondered what I could do to help my soldiers learn their left from their right, but it turned out I didn't need to do anything at all, thanks to Bob.

When I ordered the zombies to turn to the left, Bob stood at the left end of the line and growled at them until they all faced the same way.

WELL DONE, BOB!

When I instructed the zombies to turn to the right, Bob scampered to the other end of the line, where he shouted until, once again, everyone was facing in the right direction.

Ultimately, I didn't need a live brain to train my troops. It turns out all I needed was a Bob!

Things got a bit difficult when I ordered the zombies to march in formation. Swaying, they moved forward a couple of steps. But then the zombies in front tripped and everybody behind them fell on top, so we ended up with a big pile of zombies. Arms and legs stuck out in every direction as zombies tried to get out of the mess.

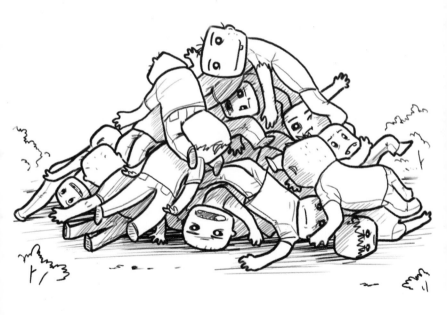

I sighed. At least we were making a lot of progress.

DAY 9

"GAH! GAH!"

"What is it, Bob?"

"GAH!"

BRUCE WAS BACK!
AND HE HAD BROUGHT SOMETHING.

I rushed to the clearing. Zombies had gathered
and were cheering Bruce's arrival at the top of
their lungs. (It still sounded like a bunch of GAHs,
only much louder.)

Bruce came toward us, holding his head high.
The other zombies I had sent along on the
mission brought up the rear, and they were
leading someone.

Someone, indeed! It was a brain!

"BRUCE!" I exclaimed. "I thought I told you to go on a scouting mission, nothing more! I didn't tell you to capture a brain."

"GAH. MEH. GAH."

"No excuses! I don't care if it was 'the perfect opportunity.' If you were trying to impress me, I don't care about that, either. It's sweet that you tried to do something nice for me, but you were supposed to gather information, that is all. No more, no less."

"GAH!"

"No, Bruce. I see how it is. You thought you were going to do something extraordinary, something that would make you the new leader of this army, huh? Well, I'm not going to let that slide. What if somebody had seen you? They would have discovered an army of zombies in this camp and then all my plans would have been for nothing. I don't have any choice, Bruce. Lock him up!" I ordered.

"GRRAH!"

Bruce tried to fight, but he couldn't overpower the four zombies that surrounded him and carried him off to prison. Bruce could count himself lucky that I didn't send him to the chair that stood directly in a patch of sunlight. You get a very nice view of the valley from that chair, but you don't have long to enjoy it, because, as we know, zombies catch fire in the light.

I approached the brain-on-two-legs and looked him over. He was tied up between two soldiers.

"Well, well, well," I said. "What have we here?"

"LET ME GO!"

The Minecraftian struggled, but he couldn't escape. Zombies are very strong.

"Oh, I don't think so. Between you and Bob, I have everything I need to create the greatest zombie army the world has ever seen."

I turned to the soldiers who were restraining him.

"Go and put the human somewhere secure. And make sure he's well guarded at all times. Whoever tries to eat this brain is going to be in serious trouble."

"GAH."

Finally! Zombies who know how to follow orders. My soldiers led the brain away to a cell. Now it's time for me to figure out the best way of putting this brain to use.

I really like talking to Bob. He's very good at listening. Together, we came up with some plans today.

"I was going to use the brain to train the troops, but you're doing a great job all by yourself," I said.

"GAH," said Bob.

"You're welcome. But I realize now that I've lost time by sending a team to capture a brain."

"GAH."

"Yes, you're right. If I'd never sent Bruce on this mission, I wouldn't have found you, and you are an excellent lieutenant. Still, I miss Bruce."

"GAH!" Bob protested.

I laughed.

"Don't worry. Bruce won't take your place. Your position is secure. But we still have a problem: What do we do with the brain? It's a waste to have good soldiers spend their time guarding him. Maybe I should simply offer the fresh brain to my soldiers. After all, it's been a good while since they tasted any."

"GAH."

"Yes, you're right. It would be a shame to give him to the army. . ."

"GAH ?"

I GRINNED BROADLY WHEN I SAW BOB'S SLY LOOK.

"You think we should keep him for ourselves ?" I asked.

"GAH!"

BOB NODDED SO FAST THAT HIS HEAD ALMOST FELL OFF.

"You know," I said, *"that's not such a bad idea. Bring the brain to my office. We're going to feast!"*

I was shocked by how quickly Bob took off! I have never seen a zombie run so fast. If I could get my other soldiers to move that quickly, we could take over entire villages before anyone even realized we were coming.

I FIGURED BOB *REALLY* WANTED SOME BRAINS FOR DINNER.

Then I heard the brain shouting down the corridor.

"Take your dirty paws off me! Let go of me!"

"Hold him still, Bob," I ordered as the two of

them came into my office. "We're going to eat well tonight."

Bob sat the brain down on a chair in the middle of the room, then put one hand on the brain's shoulder. Bob and I stood on either side of the brain. I grinned at my lieutenant.

"This was a good idea, *Bob*," I said to him. "I can't believe I wanted to share this guy with the rest of the army!"

"STOP!"

The brain threw his arms in the air and shook his head. "Why are you doing this?" he asked. "I haven't done you any harm."

"Maybe," I said, "but you will! You adventurers are all the same. You only want one thing: to destroy zombies like us."

"I don't!" protested the brain.

"Yes, you. . .," I began to say something but then stopped. "Hold on. You understood what I said just now?"

"But of course!"

The adventurer straightened in his chair. His excitement was suddenly greater than his fear, even though he was surrounded by two starving, undead monsters.

"I've been studying zombie language for a long time," said the brain. "It is interesting that you, for example, speak the dialect of the jungle biome. But the zombies you have guarding me speak the dialect of the extreme hills. And yet you are able to understand each other! Even this little breakthrough will allow us to broaden our Minecraftian understanding of the zombie species. . ."

I leaned against my desk. "Why would someone be so interested in studying zombie dialects?" I asked.

My interest in this brain was unexpectedly stronger than my desire to eat him. For the moment.

"BECAUSE YOU ARE FASCINATING!" replied the brain. "I am the world's leading expert on the subject of zombies. And from this short conversation with you, I already see that I still have so much to learn..."

"THE WORLD'S LEADING EXPERT ? REALLY ?"

"Well, Horatio Lake acts like he's the best, but, having read his latest essay on zombies, 'The Intelligence of Zombies: Or Rather, Their Lack of Intelligence,' I realized he doesn't know what he's talking about. I always knew that zombies were smart, although they might not be as smart as adventurers. And now the proof is right in front of me."

He gulped when he saw my expression when he said I am not as intelligent as he is!

"And so," the brain concluded hastily, "I do claim to be the world's expert on zombies."

"GAH ?"

"Patience, Bob," I said. "I know you're hungry, but you're going to have to find something else to eat. This brain is no longer on the menu."

"GAH."

I knew that Bob was disappointed, but I was intrigued by the brain's words. I wanted to learn more about his work. "What's your name, brain ?" I asked.

"My name is Arturio Milo."

"Art...Arti...Artor..." I struggled to pronounce his name. It was too difficult. "Forget that name. Here, among the zombies, you are nothing more than Dinner."

The brain turned pale when he heard the word *Dinner*. It was a stark reminder that he was only food to us.

"And. . .what should I call you, Mr. Zombie?" asked the brain.

He was brave, I'll give him that. Even though he was obviously terrified by the idea of being eaten, he was still trying to have a polite conversation with me.

"YOU MAY CALL ME BERN THE MAGNIFICENT."

"Very good, Mr. Bern."

I looked at him darkly.

"Mr. Bern the Magnificent," he corrected himself quickly.

I looked at Bob. "Take him back to his cell," I ordered. "I have the feeling that this brain will find a way to prove useful in the end."

"GAH?"

"Indeed, even more useful than ending up as food."

Bob trailed away miserably, disappointed to have missed out on such a delicious meal. Eh, he'll get over it. I'll find him something nice to snack on later. In the meantime, I will have to think of the best way I can use Dinner to feed not just a few soldiers, but my entire army.

DAY 11

Watching Bob training the troops, I couldn't have been prouder. He knew exactly how to keep them in line. And if one zombie so much as took a step in the wrong direction, Bob yelled at him so loudly that you could hear it in the next valley over.

Since I saw that Bob was able to look after the troops without me, I went to visit Dinner. He was sitting in his cell. When he saw me, he jumped to his feet and saluted.

Looks like this human had been pretty well trained himself!

"What can I do for you, Mr. Bern the Magnificent?" Dinner asked.

"I want to have a little chat. Come with me." I gestured to the sentries to let the human pass. Then I noticed that one sentry tried to take a bite of Dinner as he walked by.

"You!" I pointed. "Go guard Bruce instead. Get another zombie to guard the human."

"GAH?"

"You know what you did wrong. Go on, move it."

The sentry made a face and shuffled off in the direction of Bruce's cell.

"Follow me," I told Dinner. I led him away from the camp to one of my favorite spots, where I liked to sit and think.

"It's wonderful here, Mr. Bern the Magnificent. You live in a beautiful region."

"I know."

I didn't want the human to see that his praises made me happy, and I also didn't want to give him the impression that he could become my friend. He was nothing but Dinner, after all.

"So, what did you want to talk about, Mr. Bern the Magnificent?"

I sighed. "That's all right, Dinner. You've said my title enough times. You can now call me simply Mr. Bern."

"Thank you, Mr. Bern! It is a great honor."

I looked at Dinner. When he said it was a great honor, he sounded as if he really meant it. What an odd human!

"Aren't you scared?" I asked. "You're all alone in the middle of a giant zombie army. Any of my soldiers could gobble up your brain in the blink of an eye."

"Of course I'm scared, Mr. Bern. But as soon as I saw you, I knew that you were someone special. Someone I could learn from. And that's what I love. Learning. My dream is to write the best book about zombies in all Minecraftia. I have a theory that zombies are simply misunderstood. If I could improve communication between zombies and humans, we would all get along much better."

"Hmm. That's an interesting idea."

I stopped walking. We had reached the shore of the lake. I loved watching the fish swim.

"OH MY GOD! OVER THERE! ARE THOSE CREEPERS?"

I looked in the direction Dinner was pointing.

"YES, THAT'S THEM. There are quite a few in these parts. Mostly they leave us alone. It's a shame. I always thought that if I could convince the creepers to join us zombies, it would be much easier to take over the world."

"SO THAT'S YOUR PLAN. SENDING YOUR ARMY INTO BATTLE AGAINST THE MINECRAFTIANS?"

I looked sideways at Dinner.
I'd said too much.

"That's enough, Dinner. Time to go back to your cell."

Dinner had the good sense to keep quiet. He silently followed me back to his cell.

I didn't think it was a problem that Dinner knew about my plans. He was closely guarded, anyway, so he wouldn't have a chance to get away.

On the other hand, knowledge goes both ways. Dinner offered a unique opportunity to learn more about humans and their weaknesses. I decided to spend a lot of time with him.

DAY 12

"Your report, Bob!"

"GAH."

Bob stood at attention in front of my desk and gave me a report on how the troops' training was going. Under his strict supervision, the army was improving nicely.

"Very good," I said. "Now, I'm going to be spending a lot of time with Dinner. He is going to help me understand human weaknesses and decide which village is best to attack."

"GAH?" asked Bob.

"Yes, yes, I know that you really wanted to eat him. I'm sorry to say that you won't be eating him anytime soon, though."

"GAH."

I could tell Bob was angry with me.

"Fine," I said. "I know you want your reward. So how about this? I promise that when we win our first victory, you will be able to eat Dinner as a thank you for your service. You won't even have to share him with me."

"GAH?"

"For real. Now off you go. If you give the zombies a break, they're going to forget everything you taught them!"

I had learned this through experience. In the beginning, when I was just starting to build my army, I trained up four zombies. They became very good at marching and carrying out orders. But if I stopped giving my zombies commands and they got distracted by something, then all their training went out the window!

It was **RATHER ANNOYING**.

I watched Bob walk away. Then I went to join Dinner in his cell.

DAY 13

We have run into a few problems with Dinner. We tried to give him rotten meat to eat. For us zombies, rotten meat is our main food. But it upset Dinner's stomach.

Humans are disgusting creatures. Dinner got sick, and horrible stuff came out of his mouth. What a waste of perfectly good rotten meat!

Apparently, humans like their food to be fresh. Zombies like fresh food, too. But we, at least, are smart enough to know that you can't always get what you want, so you have to be happy with what you've got. Humans, on the other hand, are fragile creatures who can't stomach zombie food.

I guess this means I'll have to find some different food for Dinner.

DAY 14

Dinner and I were sitting on the shore of the lake. He was fishing for some food.

"*Here, Mr. Bern.*
Do you like fish?"

Dinner had caught a fish in the water and was holding it out to me.

I looked at the fish, then bit into its head.

Fish brain is nowhere near as good as human brain! I spit everything out and threw the fish back at Dinner.

"ARE YOU TRYING TO POISON ME OR WHAT?" I SHOUTED. "IS THIS YOUR IDEA OF REVENGE?"

"No, Mr. Bern. That's the last thing on my mind. I was only trying to offer you my friendship. I told you already. I want to help build a relationship between humans and zombies."

Dinner pulled a notebook out of his pocket and began to write in it.

"What have you got there?" I asked.

"These are the notes for my next book. It will be called, *Of Course Zombies Are Intelligent*. It will put an end to the arguments about zombies. Once it is published, Horatio Lake will have to eat his words!"

"Let me see."

Dinner handed me his notebook. "I don't know if it will make much sense to you," he said. "Most of my notes are written in code. I don't want them to fall into the hands of a bad person who might steal my research."

"A bad person? You mean like me?"

Dinner laughed. "Of course not! It's mostly Horatio Lake who worries me. There is a lot of money at stake when it comes to zombie research. If Horatio Lake ever found out that I might come up with a better book than his, he would do anything to steal my notes and profit from them. But with this code, he will have no chance of figuring out what I have written. And if he ever tried to use what he found in here, he would end up looking pretty silly."

I glanced at the most recent entry:
Zombies love eating fish.

"HA!" I exclaimed. "I see what you did there. Very clever!" I snapped the notebook shut and handed it back to Dinner. "Excellent. You may continue keeping notes about us. But I expect you to show me your notebook every time I ask for it. And if there is anything inside it that I don't understand, you must explain it to me. If at any point I suspect that you are lying to me, I'm going to hand you over to Bob so that he can munch on your brain."

"DON'T WORRY. I WILL NEVER LIE TO YOU, MR. BERN.

"YOU MAY CALL ME BERN."

DAY 15

In many ways, Dinner is much better company than any of my zombies. It is so refreshing to be able to talk to someone with half a brain! But what am I saying? Dinner has a WHOLE brain, and he knows how to use it!

He has told me very interesting things about Minecraftians. Apparently, they have discovered a zombie cure. It doesn't work on all undead monsters, but, if a zombie had once been human, that zombie can be retransformed into a human with the help of magic.

MAGIC! IT'S CRAZY WHAT YOU CAN DO WITH MAGIC.

TURNING INTO A HUMAN! I can't imagine anything more terrifying than that. I warned Dinner that if he ever tried to transform me, he would no longer be just Dinner, he would also be Breakfast and Lunch.

Dinner got the message. He changed the subject and started telling me about these objects called "enchanted swords." They're even more powerful than ordinary swords! I wondered how I could get some for my army. Think of it. Hundreds of zombies equipped with enchanted swords. We'd be unbeatable!

I must immediately create a team of soldiers who will be in charge of making enchanted swords.

DAY 16

I love being a zombie, but I must confess that, sometimes, I wish there were more zombies like me. Most of us are completely stupid!

I guess that's why it's so easy being their boss. The other zombies admire me and are always waiting around for me to tell them what to do.

IT'S HARD THINKING FOR EVERYONE ELSE!

I asked Bob to choose five zombies who, in his opinion, would be good at making enchanted swords. He has been spending so much time with the troops lately. He knows best which soldiers can take on the job of making weapons.

EITHER BOB HAD CHOSEN THE WORST ONES ON PURPOSE, OR ELSE ZOMBIES ARE TRULY IDIOTS.

I decided to make the zombies' job easier and gave them regular swords to start with. We've got a bunch of regular swords in the camp. They used to belong to the adventurers we've eaten over the years. Now, all my soldiers had to do was enchant these swords. I thought it couldn't be that hard.

But they didn't even try! One of the zombies tried to swallow his sword. (Note to self: Hand out bigger food rations to the troops next week.) Another put his sword through his foot and kept turning in circles. He didn't realize that it was the sword holding him in place! A third started waving his weapon all over the place and nearly cut off his neighbors' heads.

I had to intervene and stop him before he seriously hurt someone.

Perhaps I can convince Dinner to enchant the swords for me.

In return I'll give him a fish, or something.

DAY 17

Dinner is refusing to enchant the swords. He says he needs a table to be able to do it, an enchanting table. I personally think he's just looking for excuses. I told him I didn't believe him, and that I was going to pull his arms off and then beat him around the head until he enchanted my swords.

Dinner held out his arm and told me to pull. But I didn't.

Instead, I asked him if he knew another way I could get some enchanted swords. He said I could trade with the villagers. Sometimes, you can also obtain one by fishing. (He probably only mentioned fishing because he wanted me to bring him more fish!).

Dinner also mentioned that there was a third way, but he didn't want to talk about it. I obviously wasn't going to let him off so easily. I growled at him, looking as menacing as possible, until he said:

"OKAY, OKAY! I'LL TELL YOU!"

See, that's what he should've done from the start!

"Sometimes," said Dinner, "you can collect enchanted items by killing skeletons . . . or zombies."

He gulped and looked at me, frightened, to see how I would react.

"How can you get it from a zombie?" I asked. "I don't have enchanted items. Neither does my army. None of us have any. You're only repeating mean rumors, invented by people who are looking for any excuse to kill a zombie! And you're wondering why I'm building an army! We have to defend ourselves! You Minecraftians pose a terrible threat to us. We must defeat you before you attack us."

"I know, I know," said Dinner, trying to calm me down. "But this is why I want to write my book, see? Then people will know that zombies are intelligent creatures who can think for themselves. You don't need our brains, I'm telling you."

I wasn't so sure about that. There's nothing like a delicious, savory brain after a long day of moaning and groaning. Still, I understood what Dinner was trying to say, and I could see how useful his book might be. Perhaps I wouldn't need my army in the end. I'd be able to have more friends like Dinner—intelligent people who know how to have interesting conversations. Most zombies don't want to talk about anything except brains.

And the life of the undead is about so much more than food!

DAY 18

I went to inspect the troops during their exercises today. Bob had done an excellent job with the soldiers. When he told them to march, they marched. When he told them to stop they stopped. He even managed to teach them the difference between left and right. Bob had really improved the quality of my soldiers. I'm so happy to have replaced Bruce with Bob!

Watching the zombies parade, I told myself that they looked exactly like a human army. When we

go to attack a village, the villagers will think that we are nice Minecraftians, just passing through. By the time they realize their mistake, it will be too late, and we'll be feasting on brains to our hearts' content!

Tomorrow, we go into battle for the first time.

I still have to select the location of our first attack. On the one hand, I want to give my army an easy victory. It will be good for morale. But on the other hand, you only get to surprise your enemy once. After the attack, news will spread, and the humans will know that a zombie army is destroying everything in its path. They will improve their defenses. The second village we target will be more difficult to invade.

I ended up choosing a little village just behind a hill. It was big enough to provide enough food for all my zombies, but not so big that there would be lots of iron golems guarding the place. In fact, my scouts only saw two or three golems patrolling the streets. I planned to send my best fighters to distract them while the rest of my zombies demolished the village.

IT'S GOING TO BE A MASSACRE. I CAN'T WAIT!

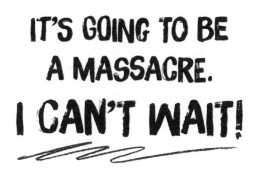

DAY 19

TODAY IS A DARK DAY IN ZOMBIE HISTORY. A DARK, DARK DAY.

I should have known that I couldn't trust my scouts. After all, the last time I sent them on a mission with the strict instructions to only gather information, they returned with Dinner. Sure, I admit that Dinner has turned out to be very useful. He's taught me a lot about the human way of thinking. But that's beside the point. I told my scouts not to interact with any humans, and they disobeyed my orders.

When the sun set this evening, I called my zombie soldiers into formation. They ignored me. I told them to form lines. They didn't move. They only obeyed when Bob gave the order, quickly arranging themselves into battalions as they had been trained to do.

It's not a good sign when an army doesn't pay attention to its commander. But I pretended like everything was fine. I led my zombies into battle, singing to motivate them:

"We are zombies, proud as can be."

"GRRRAH!"

"We don't need your sympathy."

"GRRRAH!"

"We are tougher than you can see."

"GRRRAH!"

"We are as brave as we can be!"

"GRAH! GRAH! GRAH!"

We reached the top of the hill and looked down on the sleepy village below.

"THERE IT IS, MY FRIENDS. A BANQUET OF DELICIOUS BRAINS AWAITS US!"

I turned to my soldiers. "You know the plan. Companies 3 and 15 will distract the iron golems, while the rest of you will focus on one building at a time. You break down the door, you go in, you grab the brains, and you move on to the next house. We're going to feast until dawn!"

"GRAH!"

The zombies received my speech with shrieks and cheers. Then we all set off down the hill, as fast as our unsteady legs could carry us, growling and howling the entire way.

All this noise wasn't a very good idea. If we'd been even a little quieter, we might have had a chance.

The problem was that there weren't two iron golems. There were twenty!

And as soon as we reached the edge of the village, the golems came out to meet us head-on. My zombies were as good as lost.

My first line was squashed in seconds. The troops in the back didn't see what was happening up front, so they kept going, and, soon enough, there was a wall of zombie bodies that only kept growing. There was no way we could enter the village.

"TURN AROUND! TURN AROUND! FALL BACK! FALL BAAAACK!"

I desperately tried to get my troops to retreat, but they weren't listening to me. Perhaps it had been a mistake to leave all the training to Bob.

"GRAH!"

Bob gave the order to withdraw. The zombies finally fought their way back to the hills and toward camp. But my army had suffered terrible losses.

I couldn't believe it. We were supposed to invade the village without a problem. Instead, we have to rebuild the army and replace the zombies who fell to the iron golems.

I cannot deny that this is a crushing blow. But I'm not ready to give up my plans of world domination. Next time, we will be better prepared.

DAY 20

"All right, soldiers. We've suffered a setback, but this only means we must be better prepared next time around. I've thought about what went wrong, and I have some ideas about how to do things differently in the future. Don't worry, we'll still feast on delicious brains. We just have to be more careful about getting them."

The zombies had lined up in front of me, dragging their feet, grumbling and muttering in low voices.

"Anyone have a problem?" I asked.

Silence.

"That's what I thought," I said.

I opened my mouth to tell them my next idea, when a voice interrupted me.

"YEAH, I HAVE A PROBLEM."

I turned around and saw Bob walking up behind me.

"WHAT IS YOUR PROBLEM, BOB? Is there something in particular you want to talk to me about? It's better if you wait until we are in my office."

"Actually, I think you'll find it's my office now."

"What?"

I couldn't believe my ears. All the zombies were cheering Bob. It was a mutiny!

"You see, Bern," Bob said to me, "none of the zombies actually like you. Didn't you ever wonder why the troops never listen to you? Zombies aren't stupid. They just don't like you!"

"BOB, WHAT ARE YOU TALKING ABOUT? QUIT JOKING AROUND."

"The only joke around here is you. Your time is over, Bern. You're not the zombie leader anymore. We're going to set up camp in a safer spot. Tomorrow morning, the villagers will be on their way to destroy us, and I'm planning on being far away by the time they get here. We're heading someplace where we can brainstorm better plans, so that when we zombies attack, we can actually take people by surprise. Thank you, Bern, for giving us the idea to take over the world. But we don't need you anymore. We're leaving without you. You can stay, and wait for the villagers to come kill you. Or you can go elsewhere. We don't care. Just stay away from our army."

I was so shocked my zombie body nearly fell apart. Okay, not literally, even if one time my arms had fallen off. It had been a struggle to reattach them. This time, I managed to hold myself together. But it still felt as if I were coming apart! Bob! My faithful lieutenant! Running away with my army before my eyes!

He didn't have to worry about me following them. I was far too flabbergasted.

"**FINE!**" I shouted. "**LEAVE, THEN!** I don't need you anyway! I'm going to build another army, and it's going to be even bigger and stronger than yours."

"**GOOD LUCK!**" Bob yelled over his shoulder, as he led my zombies away to who-knows-where.

DAY 21

Bob was right. The villagers came to the forest in the morning, looking for my zombie army. Luckily for me, they were looking for an entire army and expected to come across a whole bunch of zombies wandering around. Since Bob had left with the troops to set up camp elsewhere, the villagers didn't linger over a few abandoned buildings. This was a good thing, because I was hiding with Dinner in his cell.

"Hello my friend," Dinner said to me. "What's going on? You haven't taken me fishing for a few days. I was beginning to think you had forgotten about me."

"I'll never forget you, Dinner. It's partly your fault that I'm here."

"What do you mean?"

"If I had let Bob eat you when he wanted to he might not have . . ."

I stopped myself just in time to keep from spilling all my zombie secrets to this human.

"HE MIGHT NOT HAVE WHAT? WHAT HAPPENED, BERN?"

I shook my head. I heard a noise outside and threw myself on the ground, dragging Dinner down with me.

"What are you doing?" he asked.

I didn't have time to reply. A group of villagers passed right in front of the cell. I put my hand on Dinner's mouth to stop him from crying out for help. He was the only thing I had left, and I wasn't going to lose him to the villagers. Also, if they discovered me with him, they might think I was about to hurt him, and go after me.

And if I got killed by villagers, this would officially be the worst day ever.

Once I was sure the villagers had gone, I got up and looked out the window. There was no sign of them.

"PHEW!" I sighed. I sank down against the wall.

I had never felt so exhausted and defeated in my entire life.

"That was pretty close," I added. I looked at Dinner in silence.

"Go on," said Dinner. "You can tell me anything. I thought we were friends."

He looked like he truly wanted to help me.

"Okay," I said. "I'll tell you."

I told him the whole sad story: how Bob had successfully trained the zombies while I had failed, our disastrous attack on the village, the mutiny, and how Bob had stolen my army out from under my nose.

"Goodness," sighed Dinner. "That's awful!"

"I know! Where am I supposed to find a new zombie army?"

"That's not what I meant," said Dinner. "I had hoped to work with you to convince the zombies to stop eating human brains and live off rotten meat instead. I thought I could make zombies and humans live together in perfect harmony. But now Bob has left, and who knows what he'll do! If he leads his army to attack another village, I'll never be able to convince people that zombies are harmless. Not even with a book, no matter how excellent that book is."

"But zombies aren't harmless," I said, staring at Dinner.

THIS HUMAN WAS CRAZY.

"I know you can be dangerous, but that's only because you are part of a vicious cycle: the humans believe you are going to attack them, so they attack first, in self-defense. I know we can put a stop to all this, but only if the Minecraftians see that zombies can be good. Bob might undo all my hard work."

"It looks like we have a common enemy," I said seriously. "But what are we supposed to do?"

"I don't know, Bern," said Dinner. "I don't have a clue."

DAY 22

I spent the whole day hiding with Dinner in his cell. I wanted to be sure that all the villagers had gone. Anytime I thought the coast was clear, I would hear a rustling in the bushes. It was probably nothing more than a creeper or a skeleton, but I didn't want to take the risk!

Once I was absolutely certain there were no more villagers around, I opened the cell door. A sudden thought crossed my mind.

"Dinner, the cell was unguarded this whole time. Why haven't you escaped?"

"AND ABANDON ONE OF MY CLOSEST FRIENDS? NEVER!"

"Thank you," I told him, smiling. "I don't think I really ever had a friend. You feel very lonely when you are a leader. Everyone looks to you to tell them what to do, but no one wants to hang out with you."

"I have an idea. Why don't we go fishing?" suggested Dinner. "I've always enjoyed sitting down by the water with you."

"I would like that very much."

We made our way toward the lake and sat down under the tree in our favorite spot. Dinner and I cast our fishing rods out into the water, and settled down comfortably while we waited for the fish to bite.

"What are you going to do?" Dinner asked me. "Are you going to let Bob unleash his army upon Minecraftia?"

"Not if I can help it. But there are only two of us, while Bob has an entire zombie army behind him. I don't know what we can do against his forces."

"There has to be some way to figure this out!" Dinner exclaimed.

"Maybe. I don't see it, though."

At that moment I felt my fishing line grow taut. I pulled hard, but what emerged from the water wasn't a fish. It was a sword, and it was caught on my fishing hook!

"Goodness, Bern," said Dinner. "Do you know what you've just caught?"

I SHOOK MY HEAD.

"It's an enchanted sword! This is a sign. You must fight Bob's army."

I picked up the sword, enjoying the moment. This sword was much lighter than an ordinary one. I swung it around, and it cut through the air with a mysterious whistle. Whatever enchantment had been bestowed upon this piece of metal, it was exactly what I needed to confront Bob.

"You're right, Dinner," I said. "Bob thinks he has won, but I'm not giving up without a fight."

DAY 23

Dinner and I decided that the first thing we had to do was find Bob. We couldn't stop him unless we knew where he was, right?

We packed lots of fish so that Dinner would have something to eat on the road. We might not have time to go fishing later, and I wanted to be sure that Dinner would have enough food.

I wore my new enchanted sword at my waist. I still couldn't believe it. I was so lucky to have found it! All this time that I had been trying to get the zombies to improve their weapons, a magical sword had been waiting for me at the bottom of my favorite lake.

"So how are we going to find Bob?" I asked Dinner.

"Don't worry," he reassured me. "I've spent years

tracking zombies. I will be able to pin him down, no matter how clever he thinks he is."

"Perfect. Let's go find Bob!"

We were walking away from the abandoned camp when I heard a noise.

"GAH!"

"Hold on, Dinner. What was that?"

We both froze.

"GAH!"

"There it is again," I hissed.

"Sounds like a zombie in trouble," said Dinner.

We followed the sound, and I couldn't believe what we found.

"BRUCE! WHAT ARE YOU DOING HERE?"

Bruce was hanging his arms out the window of his prison cell, looking very miserable.

"GAH."

"Hold on . . ." I said. "You mean Bob forgot about you when he left with his army?"

"GAH."

"I don't think Bob forgot about him," Dinner said. "I think Bob left him behind on purpose because Bob knew that Bruce was your old lieutenant. And Bob wanted to make sure that all the zombies in his army were completely devoted to him, and only him. Even though you threw Bruce in prison, Bob knows that Bruce is still one of your allies. You should've heard Bruce talking about you while he was bringing me here. He kept saying that you were a great leader and that you would someday rule the world."

"Is that true, Bruce?" I asked. "You really said all that?"

"GAH."

"I'm so sorry, Bruce. I treated you awfully, and you deserve so much better."

"GAH."

"All right, don't push your luck, Bruce."

I opened the lock on Bruce's door to let him out.

Now there are three of us. Three against an army. Will it be enough?

DAY 24

Dinner is an excellent zombie tracker. I was surprised by how easily he was able to put us on the path to Bob's hideout. To be fair, a zombie army leaves a lot of damage in its wake. There were many clues that put us on the zombies' trail, such as trees that have fallen down and chicken bones lying around the remains of a campfire.

I was hoping that, with a little bit of luck, the villagers would find Bob and his troops before we did, and then the iron golems would give the zombies a bruising. The golems would do all the work for me and I wouldn't have to fight Bob. I had no idea what I was going to do once we finally caught him.

DAY 25

"I HAVE AN IDEA," Dinner began. "We don't have enough time to raise an army. Either way, Bob has already recruited every zombie for miles around. We would have to go very far to find enough recruits ourselves. But who says our army has to be a zombie army? Why don't we talk to the humans? We can tell them that you want peace between zombies and Minecraftians. If we tell them that Bob is power hungry, and that you are the true leader of the zombies, I am sure the humans will help us. Especially when they see how kind and gentle you and Bruce are."

Nobody had ever called me "kind and gentle" before, but I decided I liked this idea. I could become Bern the Benevolent!

"What do you think, Bruce?" I asked.

Ever since I freed Bruce from his cell, I had been trying to be really nice to him. I wanted him to forgive me for locking him up. If I had been nicer to Bruce from the beginning, Bob never would've run away with my army. Bruce has never blamed me, but I couldn't stop thinking about how I had made a big mistake.

"GAH," Bruce said.

"Yes, you're right. That is a problem. When the villagers see us, they're going to attack us first and ask questions later."

"I also know what we could do about that," Dinner confessed. He looked down at the ground and kicked a pebble. He summoned the courage to tell us the rest.

"Only thing is, I don't think you two are going to like my idea very much . . ."

DAY 26

"GAH."

"No, I'm not sure we can trust him, Bruce," I said. "But do we have any choice?"

"GAH."

"I understand you're worried, Bruce. But, as your commander, I must override your objection. Go ahead, Dinner. Get to work."

Bruce and I held out our hands so that Dinner could tie us up. He kept apologizing as he tightened the knots.

"I'm really sorry. Is that too tight? I don't want to hurt you or make your arms fall off. I made that happen to a zombie once . . ."

BRUCE GLARED AT ME.

"GRAH."

"Don't worry," Dinner reassured us hastily. "I know a lot more about zombies now than I did back then. Your arms are safe with me."

Once we were tied up well enough so the villagers wouldn't think we were a threat, Dinner drew my sword.

"BE CAREFUL WITH MY SWORD," I TOLD HIM. "IT'S VERY SPECIAL."

"I know," Dinner replied. "And I'll give it back to you as soon as the villagers see that you are friendly. I promise."

After everything I had put Dinner through, I couldn't be completely sure that he was trustworthy. But I didn't have a better plan. Bob's army could attack at any moment, and that would be the beginning of a merciless war between the Minecraftians and the zombies. Once, I would have delighted at such a thing. But the truth is, the more time I spent with Dinner, the more I realized that I liked humans. They were funny, interesting, and very good company. Dinner was a friend now, and I did not want to fight his people.

"Are you ready, Bern?" Dinner asked.

"I'm ready."

"GAH," Bruce confirmed.

If my heart were still beating, it would've been pounding so hard by now it probably would've jumped right out of my chest. I was very nervous as we approached the nearest village. I had already seen with my own eyes what an iron golem could do to a zombie. I knew that if Dinner didn't stick to his part of the plan, Bruce and I would get squashed flat in a matter of seconds.

"HELLO!" shouted Dinner as we entered the village. "Is everyone asleep?"

It was the end of the day, and all the villagers had gone to their homes. But, given that the sun had only just set, we were hoping most of them were still awake.

"I have to speak to your leader," Dinner continued.

CREAK! CLACK! CREEAAAAAK! CLACCCK!

It only took a few seconds for the iron golems to surround us. One of them raised his fist. I closed my eyes and everything went black. (That is because my eyelids are very efficient. They block out the light really well.)

I thought I was going to die as the iron golems closed in around us, but no. Dinner kept his promise. He's very good at getting people to do what he wants. Dinner positioned himself between the golems and me. Golems don't attack Minecraftians, not unless provoked. The golem waited, impassive, while Dinner called on the village leader to come out and meet us. Then the golems took us to a meeting room, where the leader was waiting.

"Are you crazy, bringing these horrible monsters into our village?" the leader said. "Don't you know that zombies are vicious killers? They should be killed on the spot."

"NOT TRUE," said Dinner. "Some zombies kill, but only because they're afraid of being attacked."

"Obviously they're going to be attacked. They're vicious killers!"

"Think for a minute," said Dinner. "Wouldn't you defend yourself if someone attacked you?"

"Of course. Same as anyone."

"See! Haven't you ever considered that if you stopped fighting zombies, they might also stop fighting you?"

The village leader looked confused.

"Look at these two," Dinner continued. "Do they look like a threat to you?"

Bruce and I were sitting quietly, trying our best to look gentle and peaceful.

Dinner said, "I am going to cut the rope binding their hands, and you'll see how harmless they are."

The village leader backed away to the other side of the room. "Are you sure that's wise?" he asked, worried.

"It's okay. You're safe. They won't do you any harm," Dinner said. He undid the ropes. Bruce and I remained sitting on the spot.

Dinner turned to us. "Now, zombies, I want you to hop on one foot."

"Is that completely necessary?" I hissed.

"Don't forget about the plan!" whispered Dinner. "You have to show the villagers that you are entirely under my control. We have to win their trust."

"GAH."

"I agree, Bruce," I said. "I also hate taking orders from a human. But if this helps us defeat Bob, then it's worth the trouble."

"GAH."

"Of course. You and I will never speak of this again. No other zombie will ever hear about this."

Bruce and I started to hop on one foot.

"Now, both feet!"

We did as we were told.

"Jump higher!"

We jumped as high as we could.

"Now go to the other end of the room, tweak your noses, stick out your tongues, and come back," instructed Dinner.

Bruce and I walked over to the village leader. When we made these ridiculous faces at him, he shrank against the wall in fear! Then Bruce and I returned to Dinner.

Okay, I have to admit that part was pretty funny!

"All right," said the leader, "I believe you. These zombies are harmless."

Dinner beamed. "Perfect. I'm so happy you agree that my friends are gentle."

Dinner shook our hands. He had kept his promise. Bruce and I remained safe and sound, all body parts intact.

Then Dinner turned back to the village leader. "Now that you know that zombies can be gentle creatures, we need to talk about a zombie army that's heading straight for us . . ."

DAY 27

It is so much easier to work with a human army! They are way better than zombies! They actually do what you tell them, and they don't drop their body parts all over the place.

Dinner acted as my translator so the humans would understand what I was trying to tell them. I was named temporary leader of the villager army. The best part? I had an entire battalion of iron golems at my command!

If Bob knew what was good for him, he'd run away as soon as he saw my army. But, knowing Bob, and I know Bob well, he would do nothing of the sort. He thinks he is the greatest leader in all Minecraftia, and he promised his zombies a feast. He wasn't going to stop until someone made him stop. And that someone was going to be me.

Bob was going to learn the hard way that no one treats me like he did and gets away with it.

DAY 28

Since I was the main expert in zombie matters (aside from Dinner), the villager army needed my guidance. The annoying thing about human troops is that humans don't see very well in the dark. This means they are at a huge disadvantage when it comes to nighttime battles against zombies.

BRUCE HAD FIGURED OUT A GENIUS PLAN TO GET AROUND THIS PROBLEM: WE WERE GOING TO ATTACK THE ZOMBIES IN DAYLIGHT!

Sure, the main difficulty with this plan was that if Bruce and I stepped into the sunlight, we were going to burn. But Dinner had found a brilliant solution: umbrellas! He made giant umbrellas for us that completely hide us from the sun so we can take part in the battle. We were hoping to avoid any real fighting, as that would be too dangerous.

We planned to send in the iron golems first, in order to get the zombies to surrender. If everything went according to plan, the humans wouldn't have to get involved, and neither would Bruce and I.

"The human scouts have found the zombie camp," Dinner reported.

"They didn't do anything that might have told the zombies we're coming, right?" I asked anxiously.

I'd had a lot of bad experiences with scouts! If the humans alerted the zombies, we wouldn't stand a chance. Either the zombies would run away somewhere we'd never find them, or else they would set up a bunch of traps for us, and our army would be destroyed before we even got to the zombies.

"No, of course not," Dinner reassured me. "You instructed them only to report on the zombies' location, and they have done exactly that."

WHAT A RELIEF! Scouts who follow instructions to the letter!

Dinner unfurled a map of the territory.

"The zombie camp is here."

I looked where he was pointing and nodded. "Okay, that means our iron golems will come from *here* and *here*. Then, we command our archers to cover them. If we can capture Bob, the rest of the army will fall apart by itself. If there's no one to tell them what to do, zombies will just moan and wander around."

"I have bad news," Dinner told me. "The scouts also reported that the zombies have destroyed several villages in their path. It sounds as if they have done a lot of damage."

I sighed and shook my head. "That's Bob's work. I never intended to destroy buildings. I wanted to create a system of agricultural production, so that I would have plenty of food to give my troops. Bob doesn't realize that by wrecking everything in his path, he is going to have trouble finding something to eat after the battle is over. What a stupid zombie."

"GAH."

"I know, Bruce," I said. "I never should have listened to him. You were always a much better lieutenant." I turned to Dinner. "Are the troops in position?"

"Every last one. They are awaiting your orders."

"Very good. Tell them to stand ready. We attack the zombies at dawn."

DAY 29

Today is the most important day in history. It is a day that shall be remembered forever.

Bruce took the villagers to a mine in the hills and sealed the entrance. We wanted to be sure that the people not participating in the battle would be safe if things went badly. Meanwhile, Dinner stayed with me to help give instructions to the humans and iron golems.

We waited until the zombies had gone to their beds. It's very difficult to wake up a zombie once he's asleep, which is a good thing, because iron golems aren't great at sneaking around!

I ordered the golems to surround the sleeping zombies. First, I was going to talk with Bob to convince him to surrender. If that didn't work, then the golems would attack.

I found Bob. I wondered how he was going to react when he saw me again. I leaned over him.

"Hiya, Bob," I said.

Bob snored.

I GRABBED HIM AND GAVE HIM A SHAKE.

"BOB, BOB. GET UP, BOB!"

Bob's snoring only grew louder. I shook harder.

"GET UP, BOB!"

BOB JUMPED AND OPENED HIS EYES.

FINALLY.

"Bern!" he shouted. "What are you doing here? I was having a wonderful dream, with brains everywhere! I don't like it when people wake me up while I'm dreaming of brains.

"GUARDS! SEIZE HIM!"

"They're asleep Bob. It's daytime."

Bob looked at me.

"So, why aren't you on fire?"

"I have an umbrella," I replied, twirling the umbrella under Bob's nose.

"Great for you. Why don't you put it to use and run away like a good little zombie."

"I can't do that, Bob," I said. "I can't let you attack the village."

"You can't stop me. We've already destroyed four villages. My army is invincible."

"No army is invincible, Bob. Give up now, while you still can."

Bob burst out laughing.

"Get lost, Bern, before I tell my soldiers to drag you away by force."

I sighed. "Don't say I didn't give you a chance." I walked out into the camp, protected from the sun by my umbrella. "Iron golems, **ATTACK!**"

The expression on Bob's face was absolutely worth it. But I didn't stick around to see what would happen next. I didn't want the human troops to mistake me for one of the zombies they were supposed to be fighting.

The zombies didn't stand a chance. They're slow movers to begin with, even in ideal circumstances. And now, caught mid-sleep, they were unable to counterattack. The fighting was over quickly. We had won the Battle of Minecraftian Village Number 23!

"WELL DONE, BERN!" Dinner grasped my hand, dancing up and down with excitement. "Thanks to you, Bob's army has been stopped. Now, we can work to build a good relationship between humans and zombies."

I smiled. "I wouldn't have been able to do this without you. . .Arturio."

"Call me Dinner, I'm used to it," laughed Dinner, throwing his arm around my shoulders. "Let's go back to the village. I'm in the mood to celebrate."

We set off in the direction of the village. But, as we drew closer, we came across a sight that stopped us in our tracks. The entire village had been destroyed. There was nothing left but ruins.

"I don't understand!" I exclaimed. "We defeated the zombie army! What happened?"

Dinner tugged at my arm, pointing to a monster running away in the distance.

"Creepers," he said. "They must have seen that the golems weren't protecting the village. So they took the opportunity to blow the place up."

"I feel awful!" I said. I felt a tear run down my cheek.

"It's not so bad," Dinner consoled me. "At least all the villagers are safe and sound. We'll rebuild the village quickly, especially with your and Bruce's help. This is the right moment to show the whole world how zombies can be good."

"You're right, Dinner."

Dinner and I walked toward the remains of the village, talking about which buildings we were going to work on first.

When I'm done, this place will
be bigger and better than it ever was.

And maybe, just maybe, I'll make some new
friends along the way. I can't wait.

LOOK FOR THESE OTHER BOOKS IN THE SERIES:

AN UNOFFICIAL **MINECRAFT** DIARY

ADVENTURES OF A
CREEPER

Mervyn, the creeper who wanted to burn bright!

Don't make me mad!

BY BOOKS KID

AN UNOFFICIAL **MINECRAFT** DIARY

ADVENTURES OF A
SLIME

Slibertius, the slime who wants to be a fashion designer!

I will revolutionize fashion!

BY BOOKS KID

ABOUT THE AUTHOR

Books Kid is convinced that behind every Minecraft character there is a story.

Early in 2015, he began writing his stories about Minecraft and publishing them as ebooks on Amazon. He writes books to promote reading among kids, using the language of Minecraft that he and other fans of the game love. He has now penned more than forty stories, which have made it onto the list of the top 100 most-downloaded children's books.

ABOUT AYPIERRE

Since 2007, Aypierre has been creating fun and innovative videos about video games for his millions of followers. As a great fan of Minecraft, he fell instantly for the adventures of this little zombie